DENT-HEAD
O'MALLEY

GUY
'THE EYES'
MURPHY

GRANNY GILLIGAN

STEPHEN MAYSMITH

PADDER
BRANAGAN

POP POLTROON

THE SKINNY
OLD LADY

THE MAN FROM
THE PUB

Rory Branagan (Detective)
The Great Diamond Heist

by Andrew Clover
and Ralph Lazar

First published in Great Britain by
HarperCollins *Children's Books* in 2021
HarperCollins *Children's Book*s is a division of HarperCollins*Publishers* Ltd
HarperCollins Publishers
1 London Bridge Street
London SE1 9GF

www.harpercollins.co.uk

1

HarperCollins*Publishers*
1st Floor, Watermarque Building, Ringsend Road
Dublin 4, Ireland

978–0–00–826601–1

Andrew Clover and Ralph Lazar assert the moral right to be identified as
the author and illustrator of the work respectively.
A CIP catalogue record for this title is available from the British Library.

Printed and bound in England by CPI Group (UK) Ltd, Croydon, CR0 4YY

Dedicated
to all mums who hold the fort
and all people who fight bad guys.

I am Rory Branagan. I am actually a detective.

It all started because . . .

. . . for the last seven years, one big mystery has *loomed* over my life . . .

WHERE IS

2

He disappeared when I was three. No one ever told me WHERE he went, or WHY.

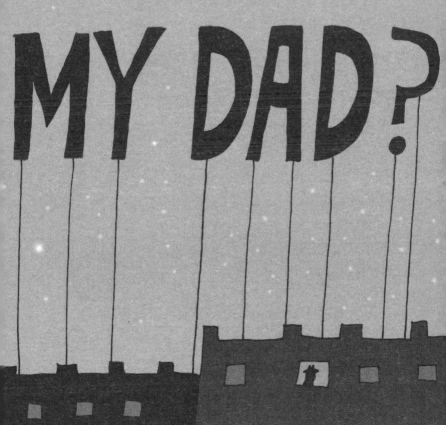

MY DAD?

But then Cat Callaghan said: 'You should become a detective, and FIND OUT, and I, my friend, *will be your Accomplice.*'

Cat is a wild, freckle-faced girl who moved in next door. She is AMAZING at solving crimes and getting us into really weird fights.

That very day, we tracked down some *poisoners* who were using *venom* from a blue-ringed octopus. Cat whacked one with a frying pan – ***BANG!***

I also found a secret letter from Dad saying he was *hiding in the place he was once happiest*.

A few days later, we discovered someone was *stealing dogs*. They even took my good friend, the sausage-dog detective, *Wilkins Welkin*.

So Cat *sneaked* out . . .

She *burgled* her way into the baddies'
lair and, together, we RELEASED THE
HOUNDS. Then my friend Mrs Welkin,
growling the words *'You dirty flip-flap!'*
HIT the main baddie with a *slipper*.

We also learned that on the day he ran
off *Dad had left me in a car.*

A week later, a huge sum of money was stolen from our school. Cat was being *blamed* by Stephen Maysmith, the big police detective.

I had to find the thief to rescue her.

Which I did! It was a *Komodo dragon* – the largest lizard in the world – whose teeth are loaded with venom.

He belongs to Michael Mulligan, the most powerful crime lord in the land.

A week later, someone tried to *kill* a dinner lady in our school. Our friend Corner Boy got them in a *headlock*, and drove them head first into a tank of newts. Then we all escaped out of a third-storey window on to a trampoline.

(*Boi-oi-oi-ong!*)

A month after that,
we found out that
many years ago Dad
had invented a festival
of car stunts called Car
Bonanza. He'd sold it to
Michael Mulligan, who
controlled the whole
festival from a tower
surrounded by bats.

We caught another
baddie.

Oh . . . and Cat also pushed me out of a plane . . .

. . . which I was NOT happy about, but – to be fair – I had a parachute, and she did it to save me. She certainly keeps things *interesting*!

Only *yesterday*, I was bitten by a deadly snake and *NEARLY DIED*. But I was saved by – who else? – that fast-thinking *genius Cat Callaghan*, who jabbed anti-venom into my arm.

On the verge of death, I had a
FLASHBACK, and *I saw Dad running
off on the day he disappeared.* I realised I
REMEMBERED *where he went.*

So, the very next day after school, I am lying on my bed cuddling Wilkins Welkin, and I'm sleepily thinking: *But WHY did Dad never come BACK?*

When I am pushed into action by Cat Callaghan, who sticks a finger in my nose.

'You *have* to tell me,' she says. 'WHERE DID YOUR DAD GO?'

I tell her: *'Ballycove.'*

And I open my eyes to see her giving me a very serious look.

'HOW do you know this?' she asks.

'Because when I was bitten by the snake,' I say, 'I had a *vision* of Dad running there. I also KNOW that is where he was happiest.'

'Rory!' says Cat. 'Most detectives investigate. They gather *evidence*. They don't just sit around getting bitten by snakes!'

'Well, you don't have to come if you don't want to!'

'Oh,' she says. 'I'll come with you.' She gives me a long stare. 'But I'm *warning* you again, Rory, *if* you find your dad, you might bring *bad guys* to him!'

'I eat *bad guys for breakfast*,' I tell her,
'and I *fart out* their eyeballs for *fun*.'

But I have to say she is RIGHT. We are about to find *bad guys* and *big heights* and *monsters* and *the deadliest of deadly* DANGER.

But, worse than that, I also get the BIGGEST MOST HEART-STOPPING SURPRISE OF MY LIFE.

It's something to do with Cat. And I've
noticed every freckle on her face, but I've
never noticed this.

(*Should* I have spotted it? Did I see
EVIDENCE but REFUSE TO ACCEPT it?)

It makes me feel as if my whole family have been perched on the edge of a big, high cliff all this time – and we're all about to fall to our *certain death*.

I'll tell you the whole story.

CHAPTER ONE:
Cow Pat

We set off to Ballycove right away.

It's one of those times when you know you MUST tell your mum what you're doing, but you can't tell her the *whole truth*, or she'll kill you.

I find her with her head in the dishwasher.

'Mum,' I say. 'What are you doing?'

'Just fixing this dishwasher!'

'You're *always* fixing it! Why don't you get a *new* one, or get someone to fix it properly?'

'Because I don't have the *money*!' she says. 'And I don't have anyone to help fix things because your dad ran off!'

'What would you do if I found him?' I ask.

'*Why?*' she growls. '*What* are you up to?'

'Oh, nothing,' I say. 'I'm just taking Wilkins for a walk.' And I try to *drift* from the room, all light and airy, like a dandelion on the breeze.

But, unfortunately I bump right into my brother's armpit, which smells of mouldy trainers, mixed with cow pat.

'I heard you discussing Ballycove,' he says.

'I wasn't!'

'When Dad took us there,' he says, 'remember how he always ate those veggie Scotch eggs?' Then he laughs. 'They *stank!*'

'Not as much as you do,' I tell him.

'Take that *back*!' he says, grabbing my
ear with his slimy fingers. 'Or I'll tell
Mum you're pretending to be a detective
again!'

'I am not PRETENDING to be a
detective!' I say. 'I AM one!'

'So why haven't you worked out
that freckle-faced girl is USING you for
something? *That's what girls do!*'

And I am *wanting* to say: 'You're just saying that because Julia has DUMPED you – probably because you *stink*!'

But I DON'T! *(Give me credit! I don't!)* I stay *professional*. I put on my hat and my new detective stealth sling, and I just walk out the front door.

And I see Corner Boy across the street.
'*Rory!*' he shouts, in his foghorn voice.
'*I'm off to Granny Gilligan's with Mrs Welkin! Do you want to COME?*'

'It's very *kind* of you, Corner Boy!' I shout. 'But not today!'

Cat is waiting by her front fence.

'Shall we go?'

'I'll just text Dad,' she says, 'to say what we're doing.'

I can see him through the window.
'Why didn't you just *speak* to him?'

Cat ignores that.

'I'm telling him,' she says, 'we're going to the park, to feed the fat green duck.'

'Why did you say that?'

'The secret of a good lie: always say one thing that's so odd, people think you're telling the truth.'

She is so brilliant! I think. (*Sometimes I actually can't believe she hangs out with me!*)

She finishes texting, and starts walking. 'I want you to know, whatever happens today, I am *proud* to say you're my *friend*, and a great *detective*.'

She flashes me a deadly smile. I'm wishing my brother was here to see this.

I am also *wanting* to say something like: 'And I am proud to say you are my best friend – well . . . First Equal with Wilkins!'

But I don't. I stay professional.

'Cat,' I say, focusing on the case. 'Let's run through what we definitely *know* about the day Dad ran off.'

'All right, Detective!'

'Well, Dad was in the park with me when the baddies called direct from the Great Diamond Heist. Their original getaway driver had run off. They needed his help.'

'So he drove to the jeweller's, with
you . . .' says Cat. 'He rescued the baddies
from an escaped snake . . .'

'Then he whisked them away from the
scene, by driving over a wall . . .' I say.

'He drove to a yard, where "Muscle" killed "The Genius" with the snake,' she says. 'Then your dad smuggled the third baddie—'

'*Michael Mulligan*,' I tell her. 'I *remember* it was him.'

'Fine,' says Cat. 'He smuggled *Michael Mulligan* through a police roadblock . . . Your dad then *parked*, and Michael Mulligan *ran off*.'

'And I REMEMBER Dad then found the Dame Norton Diamond in the car,' I say. 'Mulligan had dropped it by mistake. Dad looked scared. But he took it and *ran*. And he went to Ballycove . . . on the bus.'

'On the *bus*?' she says.

'Yes!'

We're now near the old church where Dad parked that day. As we head down the path, I see something.

'Get down,' I say.

We dive behind a tree.

'What?'

'I think I saw something,' I tell her.

We both peek round the tree.

'I see NOTHING!' says Cat.

'Look behind that fence,' I say. 'There are two black shapes . . . What do you think they are?'

'I don't know! What do *you* think they are?'

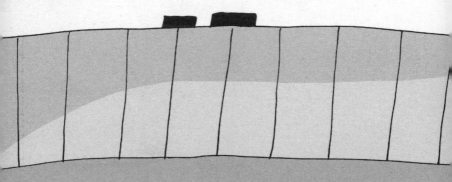

'I think they're the top hats of
Mulligan's men – Guy "The Eyes"
Murphy, and Derek "Dent-head"
O'Malley! *They're after us!'*

And suddenly I feel very scared.

CHAPTER TWO:
Bad Guys

'*Shush,*' Cat says.

I shush. I am so quiet I don't even breathe. My head is leaning against the tree, and all I can hear is the blood in my ears. It makes a *swish*, *swish* noise, which sounds like swords cutting through the air.

'We need to get away,' says Cat. '*Run!*'
We *sprint* off down the path. All the
way, I keep checking over my shoulder.
There's no sign of the bad guys.

But just as we reach the
end . . . there is.

We *speed* across the road, where we're in luck. A bus is waiting at the bus stop.

We run over and jump on.

'I'm just having my break,' says the driver, pulling out a ham sandwich.

So now I'm wanting to DRIVE THAT SANDWICH RIGHT UP HIS NOSE WITH A GIANT HAMMER.

But I can't see how that will get us to Ballycove.

Just then, we see the bad guys crossing the road towards the bus. I go cold with fear. We hit the floor. Then . . . as they climb on through the back door, we crawl back out the *front*.

And . . .

. . . we see Mrs Welkin and Corner Boy, driving past in her Fiat Punto. (*Saved by the Welkin!*)

'Where are you going?' asks Mrs Welkin.

'Ballycove.'

'That's where we're going! Would you like a lift?'

We jump in the back.

But Mrs Welkin doesn't drive off. *If you hurry*, she always says, *you don't enjoy the view.*

And I have *plenty* of time to see the coast, with Ballycove in the distance, and a seagull flying over with a chip in its beak.

In the mirror, I *also see the bad guys coming*. We hit the floor.

'Don't let those men know we're here!' I whisper.

Corner Boy spreads bags over us. So now I'm on the floor, covered up. I am just like Michael Mulligan was in the getaway car, on that fateful day . . .

. . . Except I am squashed against
Wilkins and Cat. She is so close, I can see
the black speckles in her eye. She smiles.

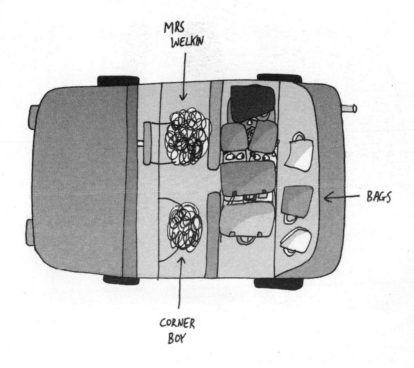

MRS
WELKIN

BAGS

CORNER
BOY

SEE! I want to show my brother. She
LIKES me!

Then we hear the quiet, dangerous
voice of Guy 'The Eyes' Murphy:
'Did you see two kids and a dog?'

'No,' says Mrs Welkin.
'Why have you stopped your car?'
'**I needed a poo**,' says Corner Boy.

'But,' says Eyes, putting his finger on the problem, 'there is no toilet here.'

'**But I could FEEL it coming out**,' says Corner Boy. '**It was like this. Errr . . .**'

And even though I can't see him, I *know* what he's doing. I've seen him do it a *thousand* times. He's putting his hands on his face, and he's pretending to be the poo, coming out.

'All right, FINE!' says Eyes, and you can hear him walking off. (He can cope with *guns* and *gangsters*, but he *cannot* cope with Corner Boy's poo!)

We are saved! I think. *Saved by the poo!* The **Super**-poo!

If we get out of this alive, I think I will write *The Adventures of the Super-Poo!* He flies round the world, solving crime!

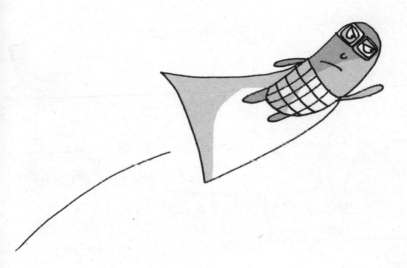

If he sees baddies, he goes squish in their faces.

'What did those men want?' asks Mrs Welkin, as we rise from the floor.

'There were two teenagers with an Alsatian. We saw them smash a wing mirror, but the men thought *we* did it!' says Cat.

(She is *such* a good liar!)

Mrs Welkin drives off.

In the front Corner Boy starts telling her all about the go-kart he's making, called the *Master Blaster*.

'The steering wheel is a frisbee, the wheels are from a pram, and I've added a special GUNK GUN,' he tells her proudly, 'which I've filled with slimy pondwater – and some of my *very own wee*!'

At the edge of Ballycove, we slow
down at a bus stop. There's a view of an
island, out to sea, and a café called Pop
Poltroon's Tearoom, run by a man called
Pop Poltroon who has a *scorpion* tattooed
on his face.

'Maybe Dad got out here,' I whisper
to Cat.

'He wouldn't have!' she whispers back. 'Pop Poltroon is a Mulligan man. Your dad would've steered clear of *him*.'

'How do you *know*?'

'It's common knowledge!'

And I am thinking how she knows
so much all the time. But I am more
wondering if the bad guys have followed
us to Ballycove.

CHAPTER THREE:
Up the Bum of a Walrus

Moments later, Mrs Welkin pulls up outside a bungalow at the top of the hill.

Granny Gilligan comes out of the house.

She looks just how Corner Boy would look – if he was an old lady.

'I've made egg sandwiches and Arctic Roll!' she calls. 'I hope you'll all be eating!'

'Thank you,' says Cat. 'But we're off for a picnic.'

'Oh,' she says. 'I'll wrap some sandwiches for you!' She goes into the house.

Wilkins wants to give me a gift too – a manky old tennis ball he's found in the hedge. 'Thank you, old friend,' I say.

'**And *I* will give you the Master Blaster!**' says Corner Boy. I do NOT want that, but moments later he's pulling it out on to the front pavement.

'Corner Boy, we're off on an investigation,' I tell him. 'How would you feel if the Master Blaster was destroyed?'

'I would be very proud if MY Master Blaster was destroyed in YOUR investigation! You're the ones who called me Special Agent Corner Boy!'

'Thank you, Special Agent Corner Boy,' says Cat. 'We shall take the Master Blaster.'

Just then, we see Dent-head and Eyes coming down the street in their big black car.

Do they know where we are? I grab Cat, and we both dive behind the fence. We hear the car slowing down.

'**I have done my poo now**!' Corner Boy tells them cheerfully. '**It was a good one – and a *big* one!**'

You can tell Eyes and Dent-head have definitely heard as much as they can take about Corner Boy's poo. They drive off, fast. (I swear . . . I will write a hundred books about that poo . . . *The Poo Who Came to Tea. The Lion, the Witch and the Poo*).

Granny Gilligan now gives me egg sandwiches wrapped in cling film. I put them in my bag. Mrs Welkin says she wants to keep hold of Wilkins, so I give him one last pat, to build up courage.

There's no sign of the baddies. So we mount the Master Blaster, and set off.

First we go rattling past a donkey field.

I can't see how Dad could be hiding there.

We pick up speed as we pass the crazy golf, which I know well.

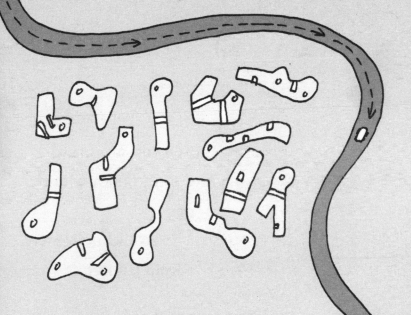

It never has the level of sheer *CRAZINESS* you'd expect. I see a slight ramp, with a hole at the end that's always filled with rain.

If Dad was involved with the crazy golf,
you would hit the ball up the ramp . . .

. . . it would go out to
sea and land on an island.

It would go down
a long tunnel . . .

. . . into
the bum of
a walrus . . .

. . . who would fart it into the mouth of a pelican . . .

. . . who'd drop it into the hole . . .

. . . and a tiny Kylian Mbappé would come out, dancing like a chicken.

That does not happen. I don't think Dad is staying here.

About now we realise that, although the Master Blaster has pram wheels, a frisbee and a gunk gun . . . it *doesn't have brakes*!! The frisbee is rattling, the gunk tank is slopping and we're *hurtling* into town, past the tiny shop where you buy lilos.

We see Eyes Murphy. Luckily, he doesn't see us.

We shoot, even faster, past the donut shop. I see Dent-head.

'He's turning our way!' I say. Cat GETS him in the face with the gunk gun, then wrenches the steering wheel.

We turn RIGHT and ROCKET – *bang, bang, bang* – down a cobbled alley.

Then we are shooting into the main square of Ballycove. As the ground evens out, we slow down. We trundle past the shops, then stop by the pub, where the bus is just pulling in.

'Do you think Dent-head saw us come this way?' I ask.

But Cat is pointing to the bus stop.

'*This* is where your dad would have got off,' she says.

CHAPTER FOUR:
Detectiving

'So where would he have *gone*?' asks Cat.

'My dad's a driver,' I say. 'I reckon . . . he would have headed to that garage, where he'd have felt safe.'

'Good theory, Deadly!'

We hide the Master Blaster in the alleyway and head towards the garage.

I see greasy car parts covering the floor. I see mechanics. I also see an *old poster of my dad* on the wall.

'Have you seen Padder Branagan?' I ask a mechanic.

'*I wish!*' he says. 'No one's seen HIM in years!'

As we leave, I see Cat's stolen the poster.

'If that guy was looking after your dad, he wouldn't have a picture of him up. Let's think . . . Your dad is *famous*. The first thing he would have wanted is a disguise.'

She's right!

'So maybe he went there!' I say, pointing down the street.

I can see one of those charity shops, where you can buy any clothes you like – hats, shirts, trousers, macs – provided you like them smelling slightly of wee.

We go in, and I find the queen of the wee-smelling kingdom.

'Have you seen Padder Branagan?' I ask.

'Him!' says Cat, showing the picture. *'No!'*

'We need to be more *clever*,' says Cat, leading me out. 'What *evidence* do we have of your dad's movements?'

'Well . . . he wrote me the secret letter . . .'

'Good thinking, Mr Detective!' she says. 'Which he MAY have posted *there*!' She points at a post office.

This seems like the best idea so far, so we go in.

'Have you seen Padder Branagan?' Cat asks the woman.

'No!'

The post office has one of those shops where they seem to be selling the worst things possible, for a joke – bad birthday cards, bouncy balls and a collection of droopy-eyed dog ornaments that are digging gardens, or pushing wheelbarrows.

If I can't find Dad, I think, *I'll be like those dogs – stuck forever doing stupid things.*

Then I see a noticeboard. 'Jack Hawkins Pub – *Rooms for Rent*', it says. The paper is so old, the writing has faded, but you can see from the picture the Jack Hawkins is the pub outside, *and there were no signs about rooms there just now*!

Peering around for Eyes and Dent-head, I run out.

A man's coming out of the pub.

'I'm looking for Padder Branagan,' I tell him. He looks round, *slightly too fast*. (*Does he KNOW something?*) 'I'm his son. If he IS staying here, would you tell him I'm waiting in the shop next door?'

The man stares for a moment, then turns away. He's said *nothing*. (But he also DIDN'T say: 'I don't know WHAT you're talking about!')

We hide in the shop. It sells fancy organic food, but the people of Ballycove don't seem to like it. There's just one person leaving – a skinny old lady, with a scarf and big sunglasses.

'What would you like?' asks the woman behind the counter.

'Could I have a veggie Scotch egg?' I say, remembering what my brother said.

'I'm afraid that lady just took the last one!'

WAIT . . . I think. And I suddenly get an INSTINCT: WAS THAT 'OLD LADY' DAD – IN DISGUISE?!

I SPRINT out.

But the old lady has disappeared. I can't see her anywhere.

Across the square, though, peeking from an alleyway like two big rats, I *CAN* see EYES and DENT-HEAD.

CHAPTER FIVE:
A Secret Hideout

'Cat, *quick*!' I whisper.

We jump in the Master Blaster and steer it down the alleyway. *Bump, bump, bump, bump.* The alley is VERY steep.

We clatter past a door, we crash down some steps – *BOMP BOMP BOMP* – then we're careering out FAST, past the little harbour office, towards the harbour wall.

'We're going to CRASH!' I shout.
Then we hit the wall *HARD*!

Another thing the Master Blaster doesn't have is seat belts. We're both *thrown* out, head first, into the sea.

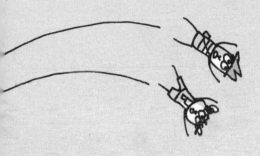

SPLASH!

Next thing I know, we're touching
the slimy, slithery, crab-filled mud at the
bottom of the freezing water.

We swim back to the wall, climb up to a
ledge and peek over.

'Well . . . Corner Boy should be very
proud,' says Cat. 'His Master Blaster has
been completely *destroyed*.'

I *can't* see Eyes and Dent-head. I can see the back of the pub. On the top floor, the curtains of an attic room are open.

A phone wire goes down from there to the harbour office beside us.

I'm thinking that if Dad had that room, he'd use the wire as a *zip line* for escaping. Those gutters could also be periscopes.

Those pigeons would have hidden cameras. And he'd be training them to fly to our house, so they could bring back information about what we're doing!

'Cat,' I say. 'We *need* to investigate that pub. How do we climb over the wall?'

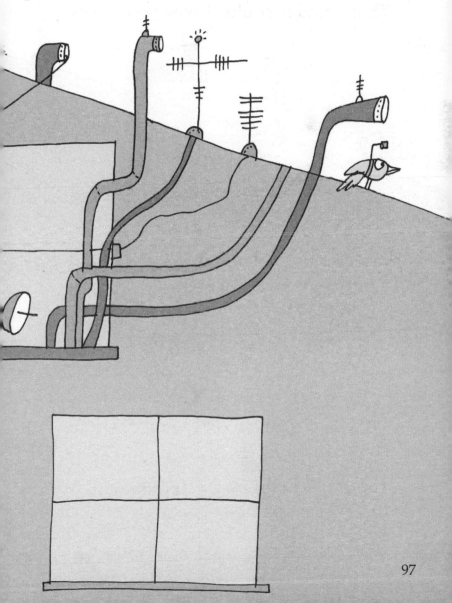

'Like this!' she says. She runs over and uses a signpost to wiggle up the wall like a worm.

I follow.

Soon the two of us are prowling along
the top of the wall.

As we pass a big shed, I freeze. 'Cat!'
I whisper. 'I can *hear* someone moving
around inside!'

There's a door open. We both
jump down.

I look around, suddenly feeling so
nervous my mouth's gone dry.

Through the door, I see inventions. There's a bicycle with fat wheels, and a car made from wood. An aircraft with canvas wings hangs from the ceiling.

The old lady's clothes
are hooked on a door – the
jacket, the scarf. I'm so tense
I actually feel a bit dizzy.

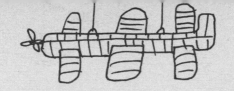

A man works at a table with his back turned to us. Tall, skinny, wearing a leather jacket. He's holding two wheels that he's running up and down a wire. *Oh my God, this could . . .* It's almost too much to take in! *Is it him?*

The man hears us. He turns.

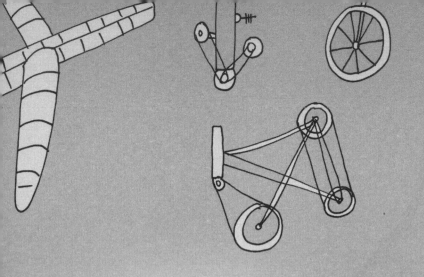

And I see it's Dad.

CHAPTER SIX:
Betrayed

'I'll give you two a minute,' whispers Cat, and disappears.

'Rory?' says Dad quietly.

'Dad!'

I run forward.

And as we hug, I press my face into his white T-shirt. I shut my eyes, I breathe in the Dad smell of him, and I *squeeze* him as if, now I've got him, I'm going to keep him forever.

'Is it really you?' says Dad.

'It is!' I want to tell him *everything*.

'What were you doing with that girl?' he says.

I'm *glad* he's asked about her. That's just where I want to start.

'That's my best friend,' I tell him. 'Her real name is Cassidy Callaghan, but I call her Cat.'

'I don't think so,' says Dad. 'That girl is Izzy Fox *Mulligan*. She's the daughter of Michael Mulligan.'

'What do you mean?' I say. 'She's *definitely* Cassidy Callaghan. She moved in next door.'

Suddenly I *remember* her moving in – how, at first, she said she was Cassidy *Corrigan*. And, far too late, a *million* things start making sense.

I get a horrible feeling, as if I'm
standing at the edge of a cliff, about to fall,
and a freckly hand is pushing my back.

'I often visited Michael Mulligan,' says Dad. 'He had a daughter, who looked exactly like that . . . Has she been *phoning* or *texting* anyone to say where you are?'

'No—!' I start to say. Then I stop. I'm now so dizzy I could fall.

Cat's always texting! And that could *easily* be why we're always being followed by Eyes and Dent-head! It's so horribly *obvious*, when you see it: her dad **is** *Michael Mulligan* . . . He was sending his men to check on his daughter!

I also see Izzy Fox Mulligan is the perfect name . . . *She is a dirty FOX.* I suddenly feel very SICK and very ANGRY.

Just then I hear a roar: *'Branagan, open up!'* It's Dent-head – on the other side of the door to the alleyway. Dad's no fool. He does not open up.

So Dent-head hits the door with an axe.

CRASH.

His head appears through the hole.

'Move,' says Dad, and we run out of the shed, up some stairs, into the pub.

'*Branagan!*' yells another voice.

The *window* is smashed. The face of Eyes Murphy pokes through it.

Dad and I dive behind the bar. We crawl to a door. We hurry upstairs.

At the top, we find
an attic bedroom. I can
see it's Dad's. Mobiles
hang from the ceiling.

Dad locks the door behind us.

'So, Dad,' I say. 'How do we escape?'

'I don't know!' he says. 'What are you thinking?'

'Well . . . I saw the wire from your window. I was *guessing* that's a zip line.'

'Rory!' says Dad. 'That's a *brilliant* idea! And we could use these!'

He's still holding the two wheels from downstairs. He takes a strut from a chair, sticks it through one of the wheels, opens the window and fastens the wheel over the wire.

'Hold on tight to that. I'll see you at the other end!'

I climb on to the windowsill.

CRUNCH! The axe *smashes* through the door. Dent-head's scowling face appears.

Dad whacks him with a wheel, right on the dent. The axe falls. Dad grabs it. He chucks it out of the window.

'Go!' he shouts. And I don't think twice. I go.

Normally, on a zip wire, you get a seat. On this one, I just dangle. I go shooting out, across the roof of the shed . . .

. . . across the water, going FAST.

I have just enough time to see a huge, black-hulled boat with jet-skis bobbing in the water behind it.

I come down, fast, towards the wall by the harbour office.

As I hit the wall *hard*, I feel like a fly being *splatted*.

But I land on the ledge. I look up at Dad.

Even from a distance, I can see why
he was World Rally champion. He is *cool*
under pressure. He climbs out of the
window. He fastens his wheel to the wire.

Then he waits. Eyes Murphy appears.
Dad karate-chops him again. *DUNK*.

As Eyes' head flops down, his
glasses fall.

And as Dad now *shoots* over the water, he's in a *blaze* of sunlight and looks about the *coolest* man there's ever been.

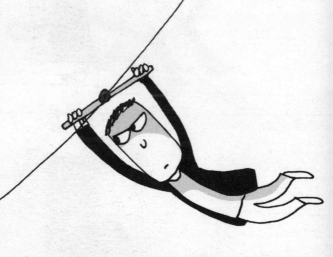

He hits the wall like a panther.

We both peek over the top of the
wall. And things are only getting worse.
Someone appears. It's Michael Mulligan
himself!

CHAPTER SEVEN:
The Big Question

But luckily I'm with Dad now!

'Rory, on the count of three,' he says quietly, 'sink down into the water. Then push off in *that* direction, and *keep swimming*, till I pull you up. Can you do that?'

'I can!'

'One, two, three!'

We both duck under the water.

And we SWIM.

One stroke, two strokes. I am a *brilliant* swimmer (and I want Dad to *see*)!

Five strokes, six . . . I am going like a torpedo.

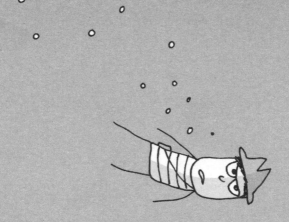

Ten, eleven . . . I am getting out of breath *. . . Twelve, thirteen . . .* I am *dying* for air. *Fourteen . . .* I am actually *dying*.

Fifteen, I am just going to *drift* up this
tunnel . . .

I am grabbed. I open my eyes.

GASPING for air, I find myself in a small white plastic box.

'Where am I?' I cough.

'What did you notice, in the sea, as you came down the zip line?'

I think. 'A big, black-hulled boat . . .'

'In front of that, there was a white buoy!'

'Oh yes!'

'We're *in* the buoy! I cut the bottom out of it, so I could hide here.'

'Most escapes go wrong at the very start,' says Dad. '*Why?* People *panic* and make mistakes! So we're just going to *cool* it.'

But I can't cool it. I need to ask the Big Question.

'Dad!' I pant. 'Why did you never come back to us?'

'Ah, that's a long story!'

'And we're stuck in a buoy, and you said we should cool it: *tell the story*! *WHY did you not come back?*'

'Well, two reasons . . . One, the police suspect me of killing Mark "the Genius" O'Gatiss.'

'Not any more! They caught the killer yesterday – Jack "Muscle" Thompson.'

Dad is astonished.

'How do you know?'

'I found the murder weapon: a snake.
Then I brought down Muscle. The police
got him.'

'Jayz . . .' says Dad. 'That's incredible!'

'Thanks!' I say (feeling very proud).
'But Cat helped . . .'

Then I remember Cat isn't Cat, and she *betrayed* me, and I feel sick all over again.

'Hang on,' says Dad. 'Did you say there was a black-hulled boat?'

'Yes.'

His face is white.

'Oh my G—'

'What?'

'That's Michael Mulligan's. OK . . . let me think!'

Dad thinks.

'Now *don't* worry,' he says. 'I've had years to plan this escape. All we must do is reach my boat . . .'

'Your *boat*? Where's that?'

'You know that tiny island you can see from the cliff? I've hidden a boat there!'

'Brilliant! Well done, Dad!'

'The problem is, Michael Mulligan's boat is right *here*,' says Dad, 'and if we swim for the island, he will MINCE us with his propellers.'

I can't think about Mulligan MINCING US.

I'm still thinking about Cat. I cannot BELIEVE that all the time I've been looking for Dad she's been lurking, like a BIG SPIDER, waiting to BETRAY ME.

I would like a BIG SPIDER to EAT HER!

'Right,' says Dad. 'We need to sabotage Mulligan's boat!'

'But, Dad, he's got helpers and jet-skis and probably big bazookas. We've just got our bare hands and some wet egg sandwiches.'

'But we can't stay here,' says Dad.
'Come on!'

And he dives down.

I'm not at all sure about going.

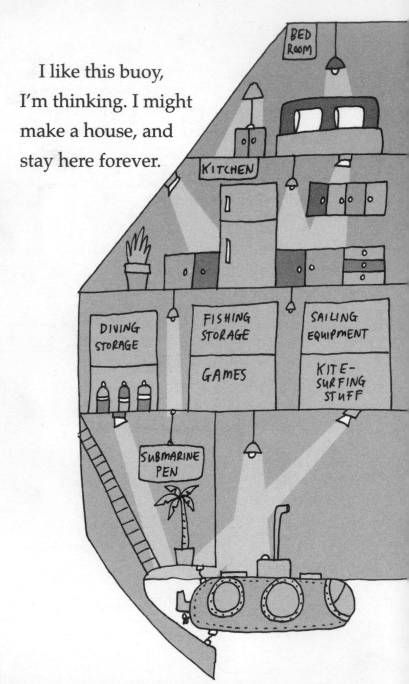

I like this buoy, I'm thinking. I might make a house, and stay here forever.

BED ROOM

KITCHEN

DIVING STORAGE

FISHING STORAGE

GAMES

SAILING EQUIPMENT

KITE-SURFING STUFF

SUBMARINE PEN

But I go.
One stroke,
two strokes . . .

I come up to see Dad holding on to the back of the boat, blinking.

'Man,' he whispers. 'My eyes STING! What can you see in the boat?'

'Dad! A man is coming!'

Dad moves up on to the boat, silent as a snake, and he . . .

. . . whacks the man with a karate punch
– *BANG!*

Two more Mulligan men appear. Dad punches one, then kicks the other and karate-chops his neck. Both men fall. (Dad is *good* at fighting!)

He looks at me and winks. He
disappears into the cockpit.

I follow.

It's like a spaceship in here. There are buttons and levers and screens.

'I can't see how you would sabotage this!' whispers Dad.

I *panic*, then notice something.

'Course,' I say. 'You could just steal the keys.'

Dad takes the keys. He chucks them out
of the boat, into the water.

This is going *well*.
But then someone arrives.

CHAPTER EIGHT:
An Evil, Venomous Reptile

It is Cat. And she has Michael Mulligan's huge Komodo dragon on a lead. I look at his mouth with the teeth that are loaded with venom.

Then I look at Cat, and I realise *she* is more venomous still.

'YOU!' I growl.

She is as pale as a vampire.

'You *tricked me*,' I snarl, so furiously I hurt my throat. 'You knew *all* I wanted was to *find my dad* and you STABBED ME IN THE BACK!'

'I gave you a minute,' she says quietly. 'And I *said* to you: "If you find your dad, you might bring bad guys to him."'

I am so angry I actually want to LASH out. *'I did NOT lead bad guys to him!'* I say. *'YOU did!'*

'Why did you *think* I was so *keen* to help you find your dad? *Come on!* You're *supposed* to be the detective!'

How DARE she say that?! Now she's mocking my detectiving!

'From the very first,' she continues, 'my dad told me: "You're going to move into a new house. Befriend the boy next door. Find out about his dad."'

'What?' I say. **'You only MADE
FRIENDS WITH ME because your DAD
TOLD you to??!!'**

Now I don't want to lash out. I just
want to CRY. I feel so *STUPID*!

'*Yes!*' says Cat. 'But then we made friends – *good* friends, *best* friends! I love you, Rory!'

'**If you *love* someone, you do NOT BETRAY them!**' I shout. '**You don't *walk out* on them!**'

Cat looks fierce uneasy.

'Rory,' says Dad smoothly. 'You mentioned some *egg* sandwiches . . . Can I have them?'

I don't know what he's up to, but I pull out the sandwiches from my bag. They're soggy and ruined. I feel I've been punched. I'm so in shock.

Dad unwraps the sandwiches and throws them behind the Komodo dragon. And the lizard seems to like the smell of that egg. He goes *leaping* after it.

Cat is not expecting this. The dragon *pulls* her with him, back into the lower cabin. Dad shuts the door.

'We need to get out of here!' he says, and I don't disagree. I want to be a million miles from that *monster*.

CHAPTER NINE:
Man Versus Engine

I go outside and stand on the deck, feeling dazed and shaky.

'Let's get out of here, *quick*,' I tell Dad. 'Will we steal the jet-skis?'

'I vowed never to use an engine again after my crash,' says Dad.

'Why?'

'Cars crash, and they pollute the world. That's why I sold Car Bonanza!'

'You don't make things easy for yourself, do you?'

'We need to swim for that beach,' says Dad. 'Swim underwater till that wall has you out of sight from the shore.'

I dive under the water, and I swim and swim.

My eyes are closed, and the water's cold, and I feel shut off from everything good. I can't BELIEVE what Cat just said. I thought she was my best friend. I see my brother was RIGHT: she was just USING me!

A minute later, we crawl out on to the stony beach. The stones are hurting my knees, but no one is chasing us.

'Look what I've got here!' says Dad.

'You have a shed,' I say, 'with a horseshoe over the door.'

'It's not what's *on* the shed. It's what's *in* it!'

He pulls open the door excitedly. I can see poles and canvas.

'What's that for?'

'Kitesurfing.'

'Wha—?'

'You hold a massive kite, and you stand on a surfboard.'

Dad is pulling stuff out. He's untangling strings.

'What was your ma doing when you last saw her?' he asks.

'Mending the dishwasher!'

'Was she?!' Dad has a misty look on his face. 'I bet she still looked *gorgeous*!'

'Dad, if you like her so much, *why have you never come back to us?*'

'The biggest reason was *Michael Mulligan*! The day after the heist, he texted me and said: *"If you've got my diamond, give it back. If you give it to the police, I will come for your family."*'

'Oh my God!' I say.

'I called Mum. I said we should *all* sail off to Brazil together.'

'That sounds good!'

'She said she didn't want you to live in hiding. She wanted you to have a normal life – a home, school, neighbours.'

'Did she?' I say.

But then I have a new thought. 'Wait, where *is* the diamond?'

'Where do you *think*?'

'On the island?'

'Let's find out, shall we?'

Dad is ready to kitesurf.

'As we set off, hold on round my neck!'

He flips the surfboard down to the water. He turns the kite upwards, the wind catches it, and WHUMP, it fills with air.

'Let's go!' he says, and we leap on the board and GO.

The wind is strong, and we shoot fast out to sea, making skippy jumps on the waves.

'Drop your feet down to the board,' shouts Dad, 'and *don't slip*!'

I am now scared to drop my feet.

I *know* I'll slip, and I'll get *stung* by
jellyfish, and *shredded* by sharks, and
whacked by whales, and *minced* by
Mulligan.

'Be brave, son!' shouts Dad.

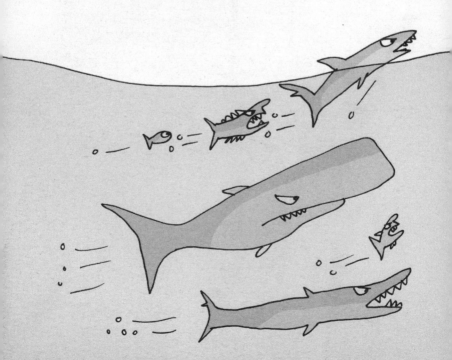

And I drop my feet on to the board.

And now I wouldn't care if ten killer whales were chasing us. I haven't slipped, I'm *with Dad*, and we're shooting FAST on a wave-leaping *surfboard*. This is *COOL*!

Then two jet-skis come roaring round the corner, heading straight for us, FAST. I am looking right into the face of Eyes.

But luckily . . .

. . . he doesn't have his glasses on. He zooms past.

But as Dent-head approaches, he looks *evil* and ready to mow us down.

A big wave wells up.

And we SHOOT INTO THE SKY and
FLY RIGHT OVER HIM!

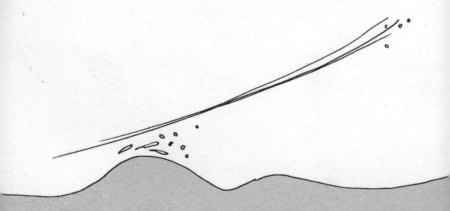

This is *amazing*, but . . .

'We'll never reach the island!' says Dad.

We turn back to see the jet-skis coming
at us from the shore.

'THEY WANT TO MINCE US!' I shout.
'SO WHAT DO YOU THINK WE
SHOULD DO?'

I get an idea.

'WE NEED TO FACE THEM!' I shout, 'AND USE THE SURFBOARD TO HIT *THEM!*'

'How?'

'LET'S AIM STRAIGHT FOR THE SKINNY ONE! LET GO WITH YOUR FEET WHEN I SHOUT . . .'

Closer! They're coming right at us, but we're pointing the board at them. *One, two . . .*

'NOW!!!'

We lift our legs and soar over the jet-skis. I turn to see the board hitting Eyes.

Eyes turns *into* Dent-head.

There's a *GRINDING*, whirring sound and then the jet-skis hit the harbour wall with a *THWUMP* and then . . .

We took them *DOWN*!

But we are now kitesurfing without a
board, and half an ocean is gushing into
my mouth.

'LET GO!' I shout, and we fall into the
waves.

CHAPTER TEN:
Up Another Level

We crawl out on to the beach, drenched.

'What happens now?' I ask.

'Don't worry,' says Dad. 'I have another shed!' (I have never met a man so excited by sheds!)

'Where?'

He points up the cliff, and I have to turn to see it.

Two minutes later, I'm copying where
he's putting his hands and feet, and
we're scampering up like squirrels.

'I don't think I can climb a *cliff*!'

'Just do what I do.'

He stinks!' I say.
Dad laughs. 'What of?'
'Mouldy sneakers, and cow dung!'
'I'd pay a million to hug that stinky
boy now!'

'How's your brother?' he calls, as we go.

We come out at the top of the cliff, by a big house with a garden.

Out at sea, waves are crashing against
the island.

Dad runs for another shed.

He pulls open the door.

'It's a hang-glider!' he says.

He's pulling out pieces. He's tying knots and snapping clips.

'We have to hurry,' he says. 'Mulligan will be coming.'

'But, Dad . . . if he's chasing you for the diamond, why don't you *give* it to him?'

'Because he's a *criminal*. I should never have helped him steal it. What do you think he would do with it?'

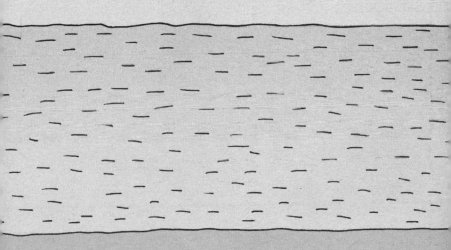

I reckon he'd sell it, and get an even bigger boat, with a jacuzzi, a dungeon, a *Fortnite* zone and a cinema.

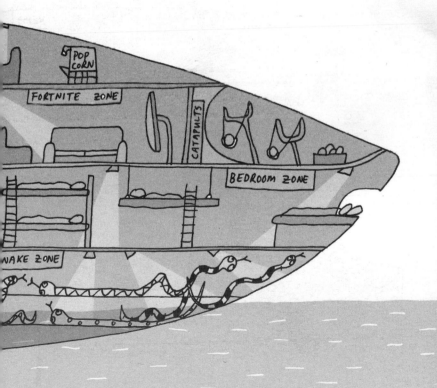

'He wants to sell it,' says Dad, 'so he can go buy his own fleet of planes and go into business!'

'Do you know that each time a person flies off on holiday, they put an average of HALF A TONNE OF CARBON DIOXIDE into the sky?'

'The world is *overheating*, and people will be starving, and wars will be coming – because of cars, planes and men like Mulligan!'

'I've been designing an aircraft that's lighter than air,' says Dad. 'It goes twenty miles high, and drifts on the winds . . .'

'If there were things that could move without petrol,' he goes on, 'it would *save the world!*'

'There's already bikes and skateboards,' I say. 'And why do people even *need* to move? Why can't they just *stay* where they are?'

Dad's hardly listening. He's connecting up ropes, with his hands moving at light-speed. Suddenly there's a HUGE ROARING behind us.

It sounds as if a DRAGON is speeding up the hill.

Dad starts looking even more quickly through his shed.

'WHAT WEAPON DO YOU CHOOSE?' he shouts. 'BOOMERANG, FIREWORK, OR GNOME?'

I don't know what danger is coming,
but I don't want to face it with a gnome.

Even *Dad* looks scared. As he prepares
the hang-glider, his hands are shaking.

I turn, and see what's making the
noise . . .

CHAPTER ELEVEN:
Battle

Michael Mulligan appears on a giant motorbike. Luckily, he's stopped by a garden wall. Unluckily . . .

. . . he lifts a *bazooka* towards us.

Dad puts the firework in the gnome, lights it and *chucks* it straight at him. It *misses*. Mulligan loads his bazooka. I *chuck the boomerang*.

And it WHACKS him, right on the head. (*Boomtown! Direct hit!*)

Mulligan falls and shoots his bazooka – *whoosh* – at the house.

BOOM! He blows a hole in the wall.
A woman, in an armchair, looks very
surprised.

'LET'S MOVE!' shouts Dad.

He lifts up the hang-glider. *FWUMP* – it fills with air.

'Press close to me,' he says. He's wrapping the harness round me. 'Come to the edge of the cliff.'

With our feet right on the cliff edge,
I look down at a sickeningly long drop.
We could be smashed to splinters on the
stones.

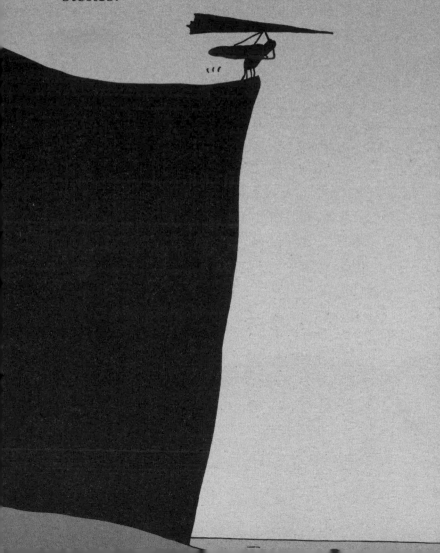

'Let's *go*,' says Dad.
And we *step* into the sky.

I cannot believe it. The only thing keeping us up is a bit of canvas.

But it's working. We're flying.

We soar over the little beach and the foaming sea, and then we're lifted UP by the wind.

I look at Dad. He smiles.

I look out to sea and I think: *Oh my God, I'm flying out to sea on a huge kite and I'm strapped to my dad – how could it BE better than this?*

Then for a second, I wish I was flying
ON MY OWN, and Cat was flying behind
me, and we were swooping down to solve
crimes, the way it used to be . . .

And then I just think how I really, really *liked* her being friends with me, and I don't know what to think any more!

And then I look up ahead and see the sun slicing between clouds. I look down at the waves passing below us, and I don't think at all. I just fly.

CHAPTER TWELVE:
Getting a Few Things off my Chest

It only takes a few minutes then we're coming down towards the island.

It's like Teletubbyland down there.
Loads of rabbits scamper around a
grassy bank. The only building is an
old stone hut.

I'm terrified we'll plummet past the island into the sea, but at the last moment Dad turns, and we land by running along the wet, spongey grass.

Dad busies himself like an excited Cub Scout. He stows away his hang-glider.

He tugs at some camouflaged tarpaulin.

'Here she is!' he calls, and uncovers a sailing boat. He pulls a lever, and it goes *trundle trundle* down some tracks.

It splashes into the water and bobs up
and down like a happy duck.

Dad leaps aboard. He pulls ropes and the mast lifts. He puts out a little gangplank.

'Come aboard,' he calls, reaching out his hand.

So now I'm on his boat.

'Isn't she a beauty?' he says, showing me beds, a kitchen and mugs dangling from hooks.

He brings out a sea chest.

'This is my box of treasures!'

He pulls out a newspaper article.

'BOY DETECTIVE SAVES SCHOOL!' it says.

It tells of the time our school's money got stolen, and Cat and I found out who did it.

Dad pulls out two more clippings. One shows me winning first prize for egg-rolling one Easter.

Another says: 'HEDGEHOG HERO.' It tells of the time Corner Boy and I found some rare hedgehogs on a new building site.

I am starting to feel very, very *angry*, but I don't know WHY, so I go out. I walk back across the gangplank to the shore. Sometimes you have to be a detective about yourself, and you have to WORK OUT **WHY** you're feeling something.

Dad follows.

'Rory! What's the *matter*?' he calls.

'It looks as if you've been here a fair few times!' I tell him.

'You can't just leave a boat, or it will get ruined! I needed to make sure I could always make my getaway!'

'I just . . . can't really understand,' I say (and my chest hurts as I start to talk), 'that . . . if, if . . . you could come a mile across the sea, to check on your boat, WHY you wouldn't come a few *more miles*, to check on US?'

Dad says nothing.

'I am *glad*,' I tell him (I can feel a big lump in my throat), 'that you were so *proud* I was a HEDGEHOG HERO that you *kept the clipping in your box*. BUT I would have *preferred* it if you had come to my bedroom and *TOLD ME YOURSELF*!'

'And I wouldn't have MINDED if you could have played *football* with me, or given me a *hug*, or, or . . . *told me a story* – BECAUSE THAT IS WHAT DADS ARE **SUPPOSED TO DO**!'

And I really *am* crying now, but I don't CARE! I *want* him to see.

'But you didn't do *any* of those things,' I say (my voice is squeaky now).

'In fact, you left me with Mum, who's always so busy and *stressed*, and my brother, who's been getting moodier and moodier, and I bet it's partly because he DOESN'T HAVE A DAD!!'

I shout that last bit so LOUD they can probably hear it in Belgium.

'*You left me!*' I shout again. 'And my BEST FRIEND has been Wilkins Welkin, who's a sausage dog, and it turns out my other BEST FRIEND was TOLD to be friends with me by *her* dad, because he's a GANGSTER who was LOOKING FOR YOU – you *big, selfish, diamond-THIEVING CRIMINAAAL!!!*'

'I am SORRY!' says Dad. 'What would make it better?'

'I WANT TO PUNCH YOU IN THE FACE!'

'GO ON, THEN! I DESERVE IT! SMACK MY FACE!'

I pull back my fist to SMACK him. I swing . . . but in fact I just *slap* him on the arm (not that hard). And I *burst* into tears.

Dad puts his arms round me, and I am SOBBING like a *toddler* who's been *left* in a car.

Dad says NOTHING. He LETS me cry. I think he even cries himself.

But when I finally look up at him, he's peering down the coast through some binoculars. He seems bothered.

'Dad? What is it?'

'Look for yourself,' he says, passing them over.

'What is it?'

'A police boat, coming fast.'

CHAPTER THIRTEEN:
The Great Diamond Heist

'But, Dad, the police *know* you didn't kill The Genius!'

'Yes,' says Dad, 'but they also know
I was getaway driver for the Great
Diamond Heist, and they WILL still be
wanting the Dame Norton Diamond!'

I'm glad we got back to this.
'Yes, Dad. Where IS the diamond?'

'Guess!' he says.

I look for possible sites.

'On the boat?'

'I'm not *that* stupid!'

'In the hut?'

'No!'

'OK. Where?'

'I buried it,' says Dad, 'at the foot of that rock.'

He finds an ancient spade behind the hut. He goes to the spot. He digs.

'Jayz,' he says. 'I've never known the ground to be so soft!'

'Well, there was quite a storm yesterday!'

Dad digs more.

He digs faster.

Soon he's like a human badger, digging in a kind of mad frenzy.

Then suddenly he throws down his spade. He's dug down to a rabbit tunnel. He kneels.

'This cannot be HAPPENING!' he wails.
'I can't *believe* it! The diamond's *gone!*'

Now I feel I'm like my mum.
'When did you last see it?' I ask him.
'*Two* days ago! It was here then!'
'And yesterday there was a storm, so
it's very unlikely someone came then.'
'SO WHO COULD HAVE TAKEN IT?'

'Well, there's only one possible set of
suspects!' I tell him.
'WHO?'
'The rabbits!'

'WHAT?'

'I can see the rabbits have been eating here. The diamond must have fallen down into the rabbit hole.'

'So WHERE WOULD IT HAVE GONE?'

'I'll show you,' I say, and I pull from my pocket the manky tennis ball given to me by Wilkins. I reach down where Dad has been digging, and push the ball into the rabbit's tunnel . . .

It rolls out of the rabbit hole towards a big rock.

'But the diamond isn't there!' Dad wails.

'What shape is the diamond?'

'Like an egg.'

I smile more. I've been in the newspaper for being an egg-rolling *champion*. I am an *expert* on eggs!

'But eggs roll with a curved path, Dad. So it will either have rolled this way,' I say, 'towards the hut – which it hasn't . . .'

'Or . . . it will have rolled this way . . .'

'INTO THE SEA!' says Dad.

'Ah, now,' I say. 'Keep calm. It will have bounced down on to these rocks!'

I move down.

'So we should find it about here,' I say. I
look.

I see brown seaweed, and rock. I can't
see a diamond. I look more. I see a dead
crab and more seaweed. I can't see a
diamond. Suddenly . . .

SPLASH!

A big wave comes in and I am *soaked* from head to foot with cold water. And I'm standing on a wet, slimy rock, and the best friend I ever had has *left* me, and tears would probably be running down my cheeks, if I wasn't *drenched in cold, stinky wate*r.

And the next moment, I see a huge
shiny diamond, gleaming in the water.
'Here it IS!' I say.

I lift it up. I can see why men would kill
for it. It's heavy and beautiful and seems
to sparkle with power.

I give it to Dad.

'RORY! Thank you! *Thank you!* You may actually be the greatest detective there's ever been!'

He lifts his binoculars, and looks.

'But the police are getting closer! And if they find the diamond, Mulligan will come after you guys!'

'Then we need to get *Mulligan* arrested, Dad – so he can't get you, and he can't get us!'

'But he's RICH! He's got loads of
followers! Even if he's in prison, I'll
always know there could be bad guys
coming after me, and I'll have to deal
with them!'

'Dealing with bad guys? That's what I do, every day . . . I call it LIFE!'

'You can't run from trouble, Dad. You have to face it, and give it a smack!'

Dad smiles, but he still looks scared.

'Rory,' he says. 'Why don't you sail off with me? In a few weeks' time we'll be in Brazil, eating ice cream on the beach! What do you think of that plan?'

And I pause. Because I *like* it. I've been
looking for my dad, all this time, and now
he's inviting me to go with him!

Then I remember Mum. She thinks I'm
just taking Wilkins for a walk! She might
have a few things to say when she finds
out I'm in Brazil. I think of how angry my
mum gets when she's stressed.

Then I think of how *brilliant* she is,
when she's not.

I think of what I said to Cat: 'If you love
someone, you don't BETRAY them. You
don't walk out on them.'

'Dad,' I say. 'I would *love* to come with
you. But I cannot do that to Mum.'

'Good answer, Rory,' says Dad. 'And when you see that gorgeous woman, promise you'll tell her from me that I would understand if she found another man . . . BUT, as long as there's one green plant still growing in this big, bad world – tell her – *I will love her*!'

'I'll tell her!'

'And give stinky boy a hug.'

'I don't know about that! I'd puke in his face!'

'And, Rory, I am so sorry I haven't been there for the last seven years.'

'Well, at least I saw you today,' I tell him. 'And we've zip-wired off a building . . . we took out two baddies with a surfboard . . . then we've had a good old chat . . . I'd say we've packed a lot in!'

'We have!' says Dad, smiling. 'And there's something I'd like to give you!'
'What?'

'This,' says Dad. And he hands me the Dame Norton Diamond, the most expensive jewel ever stolen.

I can't believe this. I see its hundred faces. I'm holding a diamond so valuable, you could use it to buy a fleet of planes.

'I know it's in good hands with you, Rory. And if, one day, Mulligan goes down, I know you'll do the right thing and hand it in!'

'And there's one last thing to give you,' says Dad.

'What?'

'My *love*,' says Dad. 'You're a boy in a million, Rory, and a detective of some genius!'

He hugs me. Now it's like he wants to keep me forever.

Then he pulls away. He goes to his boat.
He passes down a flare gun.

'I have to sail from the island,' he says,
'and disappear round the corner of the
coast. I don't want the police to see me. So
as soon as I set off, fire the flare that way,
and it'll distract them. Will you do it?'

So he really *is* going. AGAIN. I am TEMPTED to shoot the flare at him.

But I don't.

I think of the very first Detective Advice that Cat gave me.

'*MASTER your emotions*,' she said.
And for a moment I think about Cat.

I'm not even *angry* about her any
more. I just feel sad that we'll never solve
crimes again. But I don't cry. I *master* my
emotions, and I don't shoot a flare at Dad.

He jumps in the boat.

He sails off towards the corner. I shoot
the flare into the sky. *Whoooosh!*

Then as I sit there, I picture the police boat speeding towards me.

I think of all the planes, and all the cars, all speeding in different directions round the world, making it get hotter.

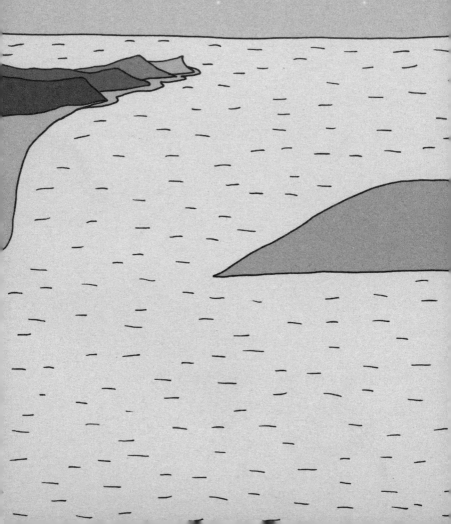

I feel no need to move anywhere at all. I just sit.

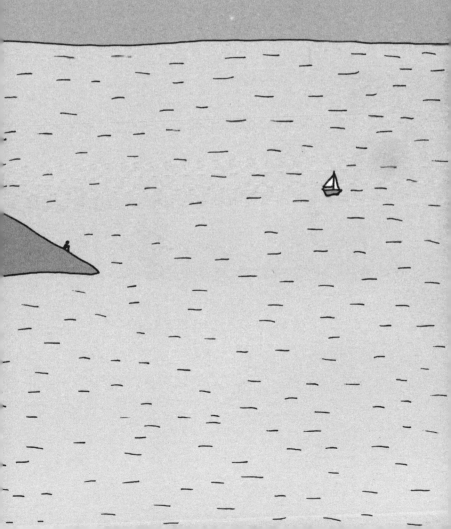

I watch the waves rising up. I notice the stars twinkling in the sky and the air going cool in my chest.

But then the whole sky SHAKES with a pounding sound – *DOOV DOOV DOOV DOOV* – and I turn and see a CHOPPER flying in.

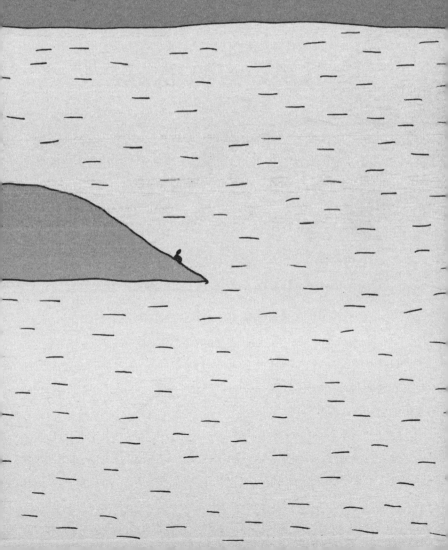

CHAPTER FOURTEEN:
Fight to the Death

Twenty seconds later, the chopper appears, hovering a few metres above the island. Its blades beat down the air, crushing the grass and scattering the rabbits.

And it's getting dark, but I have no trouble at all seeing *Michael Mulligan*, with his white-faced daughter sitting beside him.

He stares at me, with death in his eyes.

Then he looks up. His eyes widen. I know why. He's just seen Dad sailing off.

He shouts to Cat. I see why. There's a bazooka beside her. She's refusing to pass it. He's roaring.

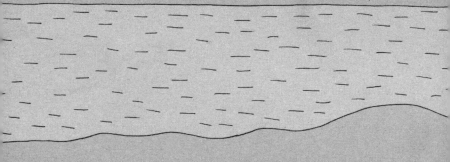

Suddenly he's *pushing* and . . .

She's *falling* out, somersaulting through the air to the ground.

She lands on the grass, rolls down the bank . . . and is still. Is she HURT?

Mulligan now has the bazooka.

The chopper is ten metres away, and just a metre above the highest point of the island. Mulligan turns it, so he can aim out of the window towards the sea.

He stands. He's about to shoot Dad!
What can I do? WHAT?

I don't have time to think twice. I run
the ten metres up the bank.

I LEAP up INTO the chopper, and . . .

. . . with a flying karate-kick, I SMACK
Mulligan so hard he FALLS **OUT**. He
lands on the wet grass, and rolls down
the bank.

I am now alone in a chopper, which is *careering* out to sea. And I can do many things, but I cannot FLY A CHOPPER.

What can I do? WHAT? **WHAT?** – I . . .

. . . leap out, into the sea.

SPLASH.

For a few moments, I'm deep
underwater, and there might be sharks
and whales and blue-ringed octopuses.
But I'm not scared.

I have kicked Mulligan, and solved the big mystery that loomed over my life. I'm not scared of ANYTHING. I push up from the bottom.

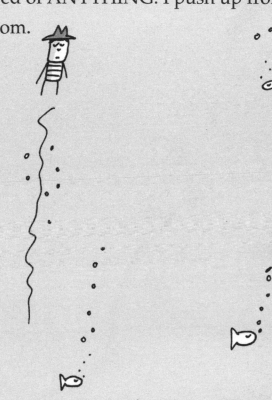

As I clamber out on to the island, I see the chopper sinking into the water, and Dad's boat is returning, while the police boat is arriving too.

A powerful beam of light points my way, and a huge megaphoned voice says:

'This is the police. We have reason to believe a dangerous *criminal* is . . .'

There's a long pause. Then . . . 'YOUNG MAN! Just WHAT do you THINK you're doing?'

And I smile, because I see it's Stephen Maysmith (police detective) arriving at the scene of the crime – long after all the action's done.

'Hurry, Maysmith,' I shout, 'the dangerous criminal is here!'

I run up the bank and find Mulligan on the grass, groaning, and moving slightly. 'Quick!' I shout. 'Get him!'

And as Stephen Maysmith swoops down to handcuff the villain, he's like a huge fat penguin diving on a fish.

'That diamond is MINE,' mumbles Mulligan.

'If he's not made himself clear enough,'
I say, 'I have a witness who puts Mulligan
at the scene of the Great Diamond Heist –
as the ringleader.'

'Who is it?' Maysmith says.

'Me.'

'And if you need more evidence against him,' I say, 'here's a bazooka, with Mulligan's fingerprints, which he fired at an old lady's house today.'

Maysmith takes the bazooka.

'And I have more surprises for you!' I say.

'WHAT?'

Dad is just arriving on his boat.

'It's like you said, Rory,' calls Dad. 'You can't run from trouble. You need to face it, and give it a smack!'

'Mr Maysmith,' I say, 'let me present my father, Padder Branagan.'

'Good evening, Mr Maysmith,' says Dad.

Maysmith looks astonished. For the last few years, he wanted to find my dad as much as I did.

'Branagan,' he bellows, like an angry schoolteacher who's just seen someone chewing bubble gum. 'I need a word with you!'

I leave them to it. There's only one thing I need.

CHAPTER FIFTEEN:
Better than Diamonds

I run to the other side of the island.

I can see jagged rocks, and frothing sea, but I can't see Cat. (I still think of her as that!)

What's happened to her? I have a
sickening feeling that maybe she has
fallen off the island and drowned. I think
of how she tried to stop her dad getting
the bazooka. She wanted to save me.

I run to the far side of the island. I see the distant cliff. I can't see Cat.

I think of her holding my hand under a work bench, as the police searched through our school. I think of her calling me Deadly Branagan.

I see the hut with its opened window. I think of Cat climbing through my window, always bringing a smile and an adventure. I go into the hut.

And I see her on the stone floor, looking so lonely.

'*Cat!*'
She says nothing.
'Izzy! You OK?'

A big fat tear runs down her cheek.

I go over. I sit beside her on the wet rocks.

'Rory,' she says. 'I am SO sorry. If it wasn't for me, none of this would have happened!'

'I know! We would never have rescued Wilkins from the thieves. We would never have saved the life of Corner Boy's dad . . .

'I would never have been a detective at all – which has been the best thing I've ever done in my life . . .'

'But I led my dad to yours!'

'Ach!' I say. 'So you betrayed my father to a dangerous crime lord – *we all make mistakes*! Your dad's a hard man to refuse!'

She says nothing. An even bigger tear plops down.

'Do you hate me?' she says. 'Go on! Tell me what you think of me now.'

'I think,' I say. 'You're the best friend I ever had, and the best accomplice *anywhere*!'

Another tear rolls down her face.

'Though, to be honest,' I add, 'you are actually a far better detective than I am. I should be *your* accomplice.'

'You have something I don't,' she says.

'What?'

'You're very brave, Rory. And very kind. And you're *determined* to the point of *madness*. And I love you for that, my friend. I love you for *everything*!'

She takes my hand and squeezes it, which, I find, I don't mind at all.

I want to tell her I love her for
everything too.

But suddenly Maysmith appears.

'How is she?' he asks.

'I'm fine!' Cat tells him. 'I just want to
go home!'

A few minutes later, we are all in the police boat, speeding back to shore – Stephen Maysmith, me, Cat, Michael Mulligan (still groaning) and Dad.

Back in Ballycove, we are joined by a huge fleet of police cars who take Dad and Mulligan away to the station.

As they shut the door of the police van, I feel a thud in my heart. I'm definitely scared of what might happen to Dad. But I still think he needs to face his trouble.

Stephen Maysmith stays with me.

'You have helped me put Michael Mulligan in prison – which I have wanted for years. Thank you.'

'But will he be able to get me back?'

'Have no doubt, young man,' he says, putting a meaty hand on my shoulder. 'Wherever you are, the police will protect you.'

I realise a crowd of people have been gathering by the police. And appearing amongst them are Wilkins and my good friend Mrs Welkin.

They come over.

'Mr Maysmith,' says Mrs Welkin. 'It cannot always be said you're the quickest at solving crime. But you're a good man. Everyone in the community thinks so. I'm grateful you've always looked out for young Rory.'

'One day he might be one of the greatest detectives of all time!' says Stephen Maysmith.

'And I'd like to present you with this slice of Arctic Roll,' says Mrs Welkin.

The big man is *delighted* with that. 'This is excellent sponge!' he says.

And I have a hug with Wilkins, which delights me more.

And then Mrs Welkin takes us home.

CHAPTER SIXTEEN:
Home

And it's only as we're going home – in
the Punto, with Mrs Welkin in the front,
listening to jazz, and me and Cat and
Wilkins in the back – that I clear up the
final mystery.

'There's one thing I don't get,' I whisper to Cat.

'What?'

'If your dad is Michael Mulligan, who IS the man who lives next door?'

'He's just some guy who works for my dad!'

'And is he married to your mum?'

'The woman I live with,' whispers Cat. 'That's not my real mum. That's why I'm never home!'

'*Really* where's your real mum?'

'Oh . . . I haven't seen *her* since I was a baby! I think she fell out with Dad. I'd *love* to know where *she* is!'

'Well . . . do you want me to . . . help you find her?' I whisper.

'You'd be the best person in the world to do that!' she whispers back.

'But if that's not your real family,' I say, 'are you OK living there?'

'I am a cat,' she says, giving me one of her mysterious smiles. 'I'll go in any home, if there's food.'

I can't *believe* this. All the time I've been missing my dad, she's had no real parents at all! It makes me see, once again, how tough and brave and *strange* she is.

'Would you not talk too much about this?' she whispers. 'I don't want the police to make me move house. I'm happy where I am!'

'But you're not living with your real family!' I whisper to her so quietly. 'So you aren't living with people who *love* you.'

'I have food and a bed,' she says, 'and I have *you* living on the other side of the wall. You're like my family, Rory! When I'm in bed, I sometimes think: he's only one metre away!'

The car has reached home. Mrs Welkin wishes us goodnight. We get out, and we're alone on the pavement. I think there's more Cat wants to say. She says nothing. But then suddenly she gives me a hug.

'I'll be on the other side of the wall,' Cat whispers. Then she gives my hand one more squeeze and pads into her house, silent as a cat.

I watch her go. Then I return to my house, and find Mum in the kitchen.

'Where have *you* been?' she asks.

'Er . . . with Dad,' I tell her.

Her mouth falls open.

'He gave me a message for you.'

'And wh . . . what is it?'

'Dad said, if you find another man, he'll understand, but as long as there's one green plant growing in this big, bad world, he will love you.'

Now my mum is an emotional woman, who does not believe in holding back her feelings. She certainly doesn't hold them back now. She falls to the floor, clutching her chest.

I get out of there, and the first thing I see is my brother's BIG HEAD.

'What have you been doing?' he says.
'Oh, you know . . . catching bad guys, solving crime – normal detective work!'
'You're not a detective!'

'Well, I found Dad anyway,' I tell him.
'And he told me to give you this!'

And I step forward and give him a hug.

The smell does knock me back a bit –
but after a while, I get used to it.

'You're a big, fat *liar*,' says my brother, pushing me off. 'I do not believe you saw Dad.'

Just then there's a loud *bang, bang* on the front door.

Mum comes out and answers it.

She SCREAMS.

It's Dad. He's standing there with
Stephen Maysmith.

'We may need him for some questions
in the morning,' says Maysmith. 'But for
now, he can stay.'

Maysmith is about to go.

'Mr Maysmith!' I call.

'What?' he says, returning.

'My dad and I have a little something that you might want!' I say.

And I give Dad a look, which says: 'OK?' and he gives a nod, which says: 'Of course!' (When you're a detective, sometimes you just know things, without having to talk.)

'What is it?' asks Stephen Maysmith.

'My brother doesn't think I'm a detective,' I tell him, 'but I would just like to hand over something I found in my investigations – the Dame Norton Diamond.'

I plonk the jewel in Maysmith's hand.

He makes a noise like: 'Errr!' (He sounds like a walrus about to have a baby.)

'And that'll be all, thank you, Mr Maysmith,' I tell him. 'For now.'
And I shut the door in his face.

I turn to see Mum, and Dad, and my
brother, who are all just standing there,
looking at me with *amazement*.

'Good work, Rory!' says Dad.
'Well done!!'

Mum is looking SHOCKED, and a bit tearful.

'So,' she says (in a tiny squeaky little voice), 'what happens now?'

Dad smiles.

'I don't know what the future holds,' he says. 'But let's begin it with a big hug!'

And that's what happens.

Dad has his arms round me, and Mum, and my brother.

As we all squeeze together, I have this amazing feeling, as if I'm drinking down pure love.

And if there's a happier house,
anywhere in this big, bad world, I'd like
to see it.

The End

Acknowledgements

I haven't thanked people, in the course of these books, because kids don't want to read about agents, and publishers . . . They want to read about dogs jumping from planes. But this is my last chance, and there is SO MUCH to say. I went to the house today where all this was written (it was sold a month ago), and as I approached, I felt ghosts rushing out to join me. I longed to sit, once again, in my writing hut, where I've had the most fun of my career.

The first ghost, of course, was of my dog – Bagheera, the inspiration for Wilkins Welkin. Loving, mad keen on fighting and leaping, and unfeasibly long, she would dig outside my hut as I wrote, waiting for me to come out and play with her. But she died, aged four – when I was writing *The Leap of Death* – and I'd still like to thank her.

And I'd like to thank my dear friend Paul McKenzie, Rory's first fan, a producer of TV shows (*Hettie Feather*, *The Athena*, many others). 'I love how Rory's not just funny, but heartfelt,' he said. 'But isn't it about how grown-ups don't tell kids anything?' Thank you, brilliant Tim Hope at Passion Pictures, who made a sample Rory cartoon. Find it at www.andrewclover.co.uk.

I thank Ralph Lazar for his charming, beautiful work, and, especially, for the time we spent under his oak tree in the hills near San Francisco, laughing as we did the military maps for *Dog Squad*. Thank you, Sam Copeland, agent and shrewd giver of advice. He brought into my life Harriet Wilson, 'Agent Wilson', editor and adored Gang Leader. I love how she never gives a note without making a joke. Thank you, clever, kind Julia Sanderson ('Sando') who works away so patiently at my wild logic, teasing out more drafts, which always expose the emotional heart.

Working with HarperCollins, I've felt like a footballer playing for Liverpool. I could thank a hundred people there, but will restrict myself to Ann-Janine Murtagh, Charlie Redmayne (CEO, giver of great parties), Elorine Grant (Art Director), Ryan Hammond, Jo-Anna Parkinson, Louisa Sheridan, Jessica Dean, David McDougall, Alex Cowan, Janis Curry, Anna Bowles (copy-editor, who made me laugh even today), Matt Kelly (prize-winning designer), Victoria Boodle, and Carla Alonzi and Dana Hallstrom, who sold Rory to Italy, Holland, Portugal, Spain, China, Korea, Turkey and the USA, where he made many friends. (Special love to Sabrina Annoni, Francesco Sedita and Gaelle Cooreman who invented Willy Willems.) Thank you especially to Tanya Hougham and Michel Bennett. (I love our days doing the audiobooks).

Thank you, Emily Hayward-Whitlock at the Artist Partnership (who's sorted several options), and Trevor Wilson and Camilla Kenyon at Authors Abroad, who've arranged many gigs. Thank you, Tamara MacFarlane, who put Rory in the window of Tales on Moon Lane and nominated him for First News Funny, the year's funniest book. Thank you, Sue Buckley, who organised several Waverton schools awards, where Rory was voted best book. Thank you to Diana the dinner lady who said: 'That's the best assembly this dinner hall has seen,' (and presented me with peach crumble).

Where do you get your ideas from? People always ask that. I don't know, and I don't want to know. When I first wrote Rory, I thought: I should imagine him voiced by the performer I most love – and that's the hilarious, big-hearted Dublin comic, Jason Byrne. (Thank you, Jason!) Only after a year of writing did I think: my best childhood friends (at the European School of Luxembourg) were all Irish: Julian Hopkins, Trevor Hearfield and, especially, Gavin Loughrey. (Is it too late to thank you, and your mums, for all the fun?)

I'd been offered a Proper Job as a teacher just before I started writing this, but my wife, Livy (just offered the job of Head of Play at Lego), said: 'You don't need to earn money. Stay home and do what you want to do.' So I wrote Rory! Thank you,

Liv! Thank you to my wonderful daughters – Iris (wildly imaginative like Rory), Grace (who helped with plotting), and Cat (who heard drafts, always laughing, or crying, at the right bits).

I thank inspirational writer friends, especially Lisa Jewell, Lauren St John, Lisa Thompson, Tobin Anderson, Adam Baron, Cressida Cowell, Jewel Kilcher, David Walliams and Alison McGhee. Thank you Piers Torday and Keeley Hawes for your sweet words. But, most of all, I thank all the wild kids, their parents and teachers, who've helped this project (especially Chris Roynon, Ingrid Bennett and all heads in Cornwall – the place I've had the most fun)!

Only today, I received a letter from a mother named Penny, who wrote to say 'my eight-year-old son got your book free in a magazine and you're now his favourite author and his teacher stopped me yesterday to say how well his reading has come on . . . ' I love to hear this. And I love to see pictures of kids reading, especially the one who went to World Book Day dressed as the Deadly Dinner Lady.

I love Anne Everall, who tours with me as I do school shows. I wish I could thank by name the dinner lady who gave me the original idea for the first book that I wrote – *The Deadly Dinner Lady*. (I was onstage, in a dinner hall, and her face appeared behind me, at a window. 'She looks like she wants to GET me!' I said to the kids, and we invented a story about a dinner lady attacking with forks and knives, and hot pies . . . The dinner lady came on at the end and took a bow. She also – for reasons I can't remember – slapped me with a giant spoon. Thank you for that!)

I thank all people who've made an effort to review online, especially Charlie Stevenson, who's done it every time. (Makes all the difference to us authors, and to prospective buyers!) I thank Form 7RO1 at St Simon Stock (Isiah, Zuza, James, Vinny . . .) who heard this last story, clapped at the end, and gave such good advice.

I thank all friends who've helped, especially Larissa Avery, Penny Nagle and Amanda Lockhart, who arranged a school visit, put me up, and let me read to her son Freddie (after he'd shown me his most treasured things – six shark teeth). Thank you to Freddie, who followed me to my car as I was about to leave, said shyly, 'I've really enjoyed your visit, and I'd like to give you this,' – and gave me a shark tooth. He gave me his most treasured thing, and I've given you mine: the story of Rory and Cat. I still think of them as real, and I'd like to thank them for whispering their story into my head. Thank you, Cat. Thank you, Wilkins. Thank you, Rory. Thank you for trusting me with your tale. I'm missing you already.

**Discover where Rory's
adventures began
in Book 1 ...**

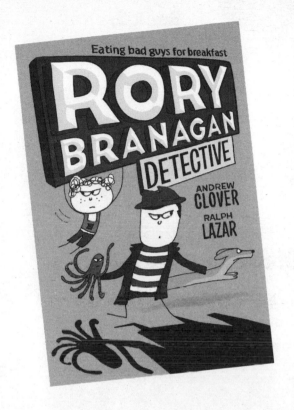

People always say: 'How do you become a
detective?' and I say: 'Ahhh, you don't just
suddenly find yourself *sneaking* up on baddies,
or *chasing* them, or *fighting them*, or living a life of
constant deadly danger – you have to WANT it. So
why did *I* want it? I just wanted to find my dad.

And I will – but first I have to track down
some POISONERS!

Book 2:
The Dog Squad

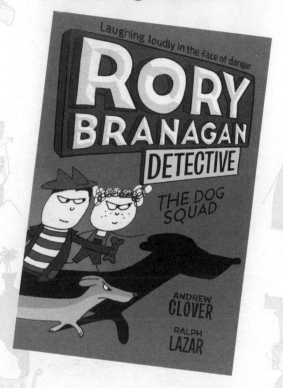

I, Rory Branagan, have uncovered a crime *right where I live*. Some *flip-flaps* are STEALING dogs. I am going to work out *who* they are and I am going to *stop* them, because I love *all* dogs. But the dog I love most, by about a *million miles*, is Wilkins Welkin, and he is in DANGER.

Book 3:
The Big Cash Robbery

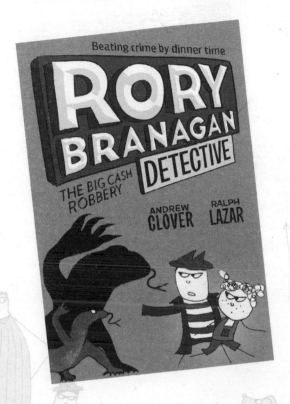

This week we had the biggest, *best* school fete of all time. We had *bouncy castles, sumo wrestling* and a real live *Komodo dragon*. We earned *loads* of money, but then some evil *thief* stole it! So it's up to me to find out *who* – and nobody will stop me, not even a DRAGON!

Book 4:
The Deadly Dinner Lady

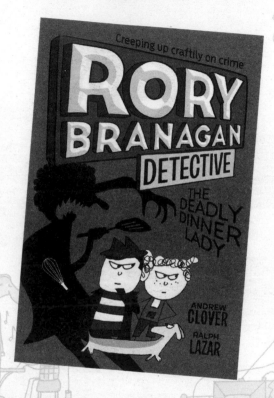

My school is having a talent show – with Mr Bolton's *ridiculous* rap, Mr Meeton's *epic* guitar solos and my friend Cat's amazing dance – but, *right* in the middle of it, there is the DEADLIEST crime in the history of our school. I have to find out *who* did it and *why* – before they strike again!

Book 5:
The Leap of Death

I'm at a stunt festival called Car Bonanza and it is EPIC. People are *driving down cliffs*, leaping over tanks filled with *crocodiles* and *jumping* out of planes! But then – DISASTER – someone *messes* with a car and the stuntman CRASHES. *Who* tried to kill him? I must find out QUICK!

Book 6:
The Den of Danger

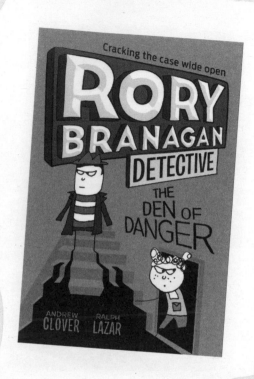

My dad disappeared seven years ago and I am
SO CLOSE to finding him, but then Cat and I get
stuck in the DEADLIEST of DEADLY DANGERS.
There are *bad guys*, a secret room and lethal
creatures with *sharp, venomous teeth!* To find Dad,
we must solve our BIGGEST CRIME YET. I'll tell
you the whole story . . .